Fang and Stinger

An Arachnid Story

By Conrad J. Storad • Illustrated by Nathaniel P. Jensen

To my parents, Conrad and Mary Ann, and my in-laws,
Gene and Fran. Thank you for all the love and support
you show to me and all of our family members.

– *Conrad J. Storad*

Rick Culleton — you dared to learn beyond stick figures

– *Nathaniel Jensen*

Text copyright © 2012 by Conrad J. Storad
Illustrations copyright © 2012 by Nathaniel P. Jensen
Owl photograph copyright © 2012 by Rick and Nora Bowers
Arachnid photogrpahs Audrey Snider-Bell/Shutterstock.com
Wasp photograph Adam Overbey/Shutterstock.com

For further information, write to
Bobolink Media, Inc., Fallbrook, CA
www.bobolinkmedia.com

The illustrations were rendered in watercolor on Arches paper
The text type was set in Worcester
The display type was set in Springfield
Composed in the United States of America
Graphic layout by Nathaniel Jensen and Tony Kasovich
Production supervision by Steve Coppock

Printed in Malaysia   First impression
                          Second printing

ISBN: 1-891795-63-5–Hardcover   ISBN: 1-891795-64-3–Softcover

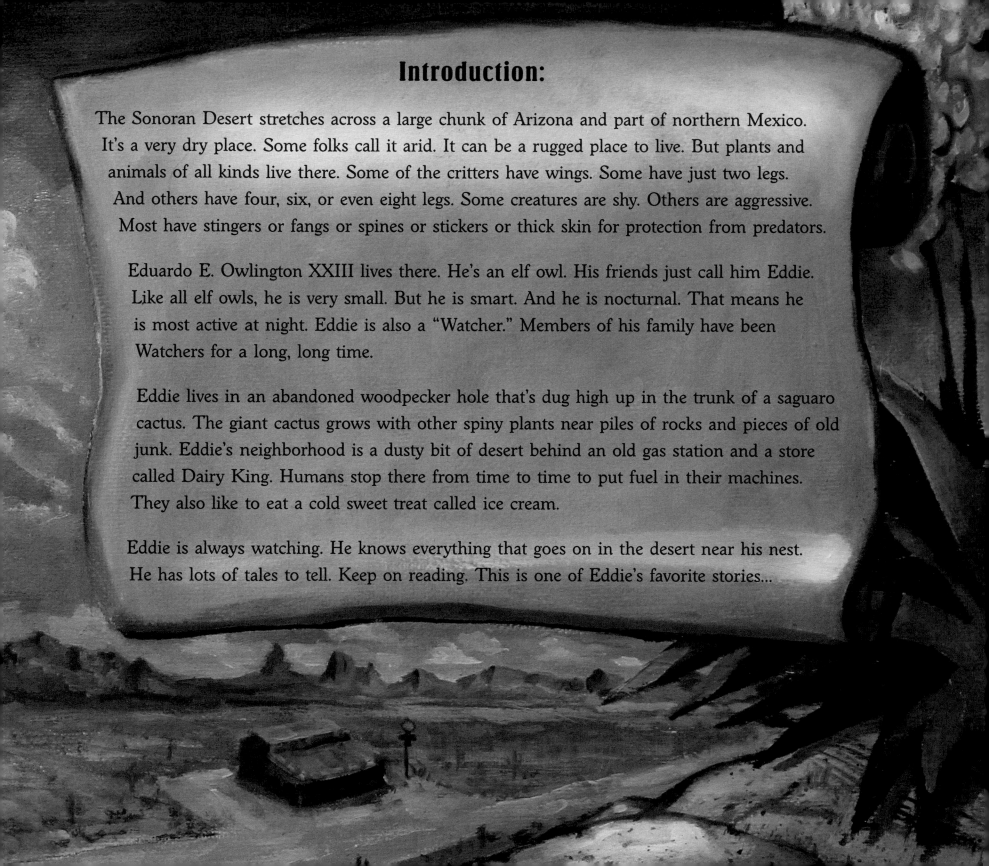

Introduction:

The Sonoran Desert stretches across a large chunk of Arizona and part of northern Mexico. It's a very dry place. Some folks call it arid. It can be a rugged place to live. But plants and animals of all kinds live there. Some of the critters have wings. Some have just two legs. And others have four, six, or even eight legs. Some creatures are shy. Others are aggressive. Most have stingers or fangs or spines or stickers or thick skin for protection from predators.

Eduardo E. Owlington XXIII lives there. He's an elf owl. His friends just call him Eddie. Like all elf owls, he is very small. But he is smart. And he is nocturnal. That means he is most active at night. Eddie is also a "Watcher." Members of his family have been Watchers for a long, long time.

Eddie lives in an abandoned woodpecker hole that's dug high up in the trunk of a saguaro cactus. The giant cactus grows with other spiny plants near piles of rocks and pieces of old junk. Eddie's neighborhood is a dusty bit of desert behind an old gas station and a store called Dairy King. Humans stop there from time to time to put fuel in their machines. They also like to eat a cold sweet treat called ice cream.

Eddie is always watching. He knows everything that goes on in the desert near his nest. He has lots of tales to tell. Keep on reading. This is one of Eddie's favorite stories...

Hi kids, my name's Eddie
Come closer, so you can hear
My story is about two arachnid friends
And how they faced their fear.

I'm a Sonoran Desert elf owl
High in a big saguaro is my nest
The cactus grows near Dairy King
Come closer, hear the rest.

This tale is about two great pals
Both are different, you might say
They once got teased and taunted
They got bullied every day.

It's not easy being different
Some days you feel just like a fool
I say think "unique" instead
Being different can be cool!

Hairyette is a desert scorpion
She's as skinny as a rail
The girl has two big strong pincers
But she was afraid of her own tail.

Some critters liked to tease her
Their words hurt her feelings, bad
"Hey Stinger, watch your tail!" they'd yell
Down drooped her tail. So sad.

Tootie's a red-knee tarantula
She's Hairyette's best friend
Little Tootie only had one fang
Would the taunting never end?

Peppi T-Hawk is a big old wasp
There's not a mean thing she won't do
Peppi's the worst bully of them all
She's nasty through and through.

Old Peppi has bright orange wings
A shiny body that's blue-black
She taunts young spiders with her stinger
Says, "Someday, you'll be my snack!"

Tootie lives in a burrow beneath the rocks
That's what most tarantulas do
Hairyette lives under a pile of wood
I swear all this is true!

Both the friends are super shy
As bug hunters, not the best
Now listen up! Don't miss this
You won't believe the rest.

Most spiders like the taste of flies
Scorpions find worms a tasty treat
But not these two arachnid pals
They liked ice cream best to eat!

They slurped melted chocolate and vanilla
Ate strawberry, peach, banana, too
They sipped from leaky cartons behind the store
Yummm. So much better than bug stew!

Now time goes by and creatures change
Little spiders grow up as well
Tootie's red knees just got brighter
My gosh, she sure looked swell.

Now Hairyette just got smarter
She'd often pause to think
"My sharp stinger isn't all that bad!"
Her "tail fear" seemed to shrink.

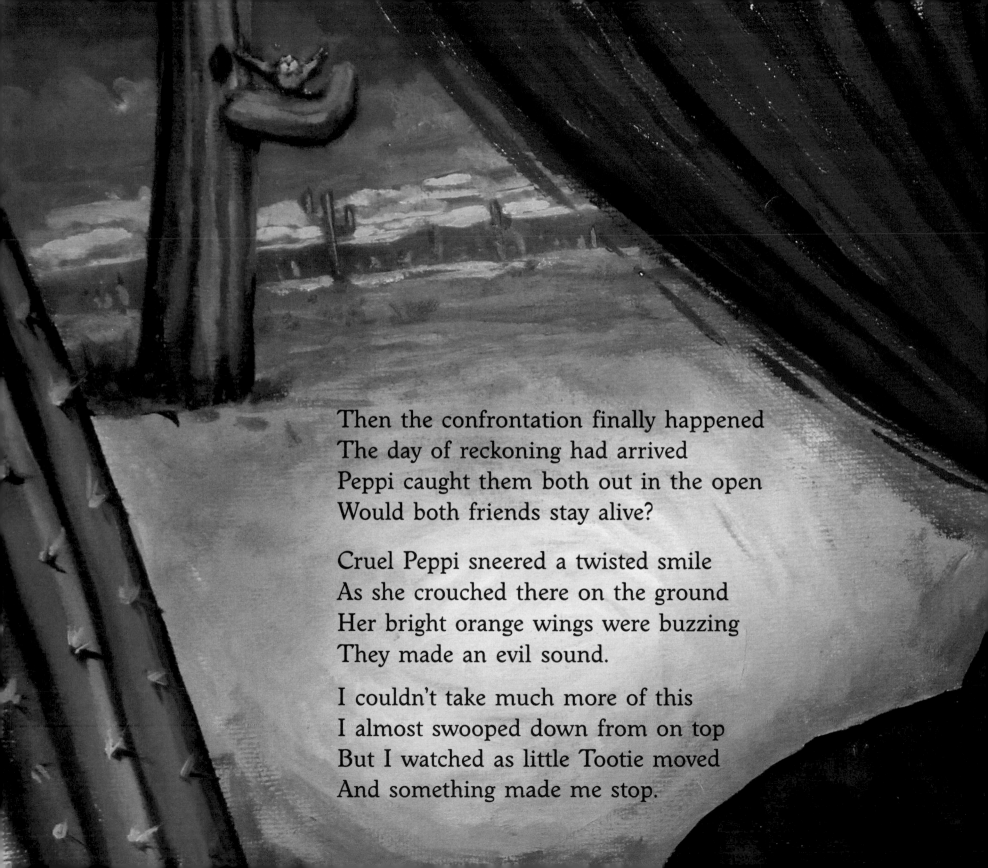

Then the confrontation finally happened
The day of reckoning had arrived
Peppi caught them both out in the open
Would both friends stay alive?

Cruel Peppi sneered a twisted smile
As she crouched there on the ground
Her bright orange wings were buzzing
They made an evil sound.

I couldn't take much more of this
I almost swooped down from on top
But I watched as little Tootie moved
And something made me stop.

Tootie winked at Hairyette
Her good friend winked right back
The moment of truth was finally here
The big wasp might attack.

"It's best not to run," said Tootie
No, never run away
Running only does one thing
Running makes you prey.

Tootie reared back to bare her fang
Not much else that she could do
But her one sharp fang was not alone
Surprise, now there were two!

Hairyette arched her long curved tail
Her stinger gleamed brightly in the sun
Peppi's orange wings stopped their buzzing
It was the T-Hawk's turn to run!

The friends stood close together
Faced mean Peppi eye to eye
The old bully's sneer wilted fast
She looked like she might cry.

The big wasp flew off quickly
Buzzed high up into the sky
And she never bothered the friends again
Not once. And that's no lie!

Are there lessons in my story?
Yes! I think one or two.
Remember, "Courage comes from within
And to your friends be true!"

Being different is not a bad thing
The friends now know that it's okay.
Heck. They live behind the Dairy King
Where they eat ice cream every day!

Fang and Stinger Fun Facts

Some spiders are smaller than the head of a pin. The biggest tarantula would easily spread across a dinner plate.

Tarantulas are colorful spiders. Some have red knees or orange legs. Some have blue bodies. Some have pink toes.

A baby tarantula is called a spiderling.

A group of scorpions is called a cyclone.

A baby scorpion is called a scorpling.

The scientific name for the tarantula hawk is Hemipepsis wasp. There are several kinds. Some can grow almost 2 inches long. The bigger the wasp, the bigger the spider it will hunt.

Tarantula hawk wasps have very long stingers. The sting of this wasp is said to be one of the most painful of all insect stings for a human.

The elf owl is the smallest of all owls living in Southwestern deserts. It stands only 5 to 6 inches tall from the top of its head to the tip of its tail feathers. That is about as long as a brand new pencil.

Elf owls have bright yellow eyes and white eyebrows.

The tiny eggs of an elf owl are the size of jellybeans.

A group of owls is called a parliament.

A baby owl is called an owlet.

Fang and Stinger Fast Facts

 Arachnids and insects are creatures called ectotherms. Their body temperature does not stay the same the way that a human's does. Their body temperature changes along with the outside air temperature. Some people refer to ectotherms as "cold-blooded animals."

 Tarantulas and scorpions are arachnids. There are hundreds of thousands of kinds of arachnids. Trillions of individual arachnids live on the Earth today.

 All arachnids have four pairs of jointed legs. Their bodies are made of two main parts: cephalothorax and abdomen. They live by sucking the life out of their prey. Ticks and mites are also arachnids.

 All spiders are arachnids. All arachnids are not spiders.

 There are more than 800 known species of tarantulas. Most are very shy creatures. Tarantulas live only in North, Central, and South America.

 A tarantula-hawk wasp is an insect. There are more than 1 million known kinds of insects. Scientists think there are millions of more types of insects yet to be discovered. They live in every habitat on our planet. Trillions and trillions of individual insects live on the Earth at any given moment.

 An insect's skeleton is on the outside of its body. It's called an exoskeleton. An insect body has three main parts: head, thorax, and abdomen. Every insect has three pairs of jointed legs.

 Most insects have two pairs of wings. Some have only one. Some are wingless.

 Arachnids and insects grow by shedding their hard outside skin. The process is called molting.

The Friends

Name: Tootie – A Red Knee Tarantula

Nickname: "Fang" – A nickname she does not like at all

Size: 4 inches from leg tip to leg tip

Color: Velvet black with bright patches of reddish-orange on the legs

Favorite Foods: Ice cream of all flavors. Insects and grub worms, when she must

Habitat: Dry desert soil and rocky scrubland

Tootie the red knee tarantula lives underground in a silk-lined burrow. The entrance is hidden by a pile of rocks. The rock pile spreads out behind a gas station and a Dairy King located on an old desert road. The humans in the store sell ice cream. Tootie is a young spider with only one fang. Her second fang has yet to grow in. That makes it tough for her to catch food. Sometimes she crawls among the leaky boxes behind the store. She sips the melting ice cream that the humans have thrown way. Tootie likes all flavors, but especially vanilla and chocolate.

Most tarantulas are shy creatures. Tootie is very shy. Some of the critters in the neighborhood tease her. They call her "Fang." She does not like that nickname. Tootie's best friend is Hairyette the desert scorpion. She lives close by under an old piece of wood.

The Friends

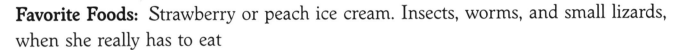

Name: Hairyette - A Desert Hairy Scorpion

Nickname: "Stinger" - A nickname she does not like at all

Size: 5 inches long from head to tip of tail

Color: Light brown or black body segments rimmed in pale yellow. Legs, tail, and pincers pale yellow. Short, stiff, dark brown hairs on legs and pincers

Favorite Foods: Strawberry or peach ice cream. Insects, worms, and small lizards, when she really has to eat

Habitat: Dry desert soil and rocky scrubland

Hairyette is a desert hairy scorpion. Members of her family are the biggest scorpions living in the Sonoran Desert. She looks fierce with her two powerful pincers and long curved tail. At the end of her tail is a sharp, hollow stinger. The tail tip is filled with venom. The venom is used to catch bugs for food, or to defend against predators. Hairyette is afraid of her stinger. She's not sure that she ever wants to use it. Other creatures tease her. They call her "Stinger" because she is afraid of her own tail. She does not like being teased.

Hairyette lives under an old piece of wood. It sits near the rocks close to Tootie the red-knee tarantula's underground burrow. Tootie is her best friend. They both love to slurp melting ice cream from cartons tossed into the trash behind the Dairy King.

The Watcher

Name: Eduardo E. Owlington XXIII –
A Sonoran Desert Elf Owl

Nickname: "Eddie"

Size: 5 inches, top of head to tip of tail feathers

Color: Yellow eyes. White eyebrows. Body is
streaked with tan and white

Favorite Foods: Large insects, moths, small lizards,
centipedes

Habitat: Places where the giant saguaro cactus grows

Eduardo E. Owlington XXIII comes from a long
line of elf owls, the smallest of all owls living in the
Sonoran Desert. They are "Watchers. "The males of the
Owlington family are always named Eduardo. He has no idea why that is so.
He prefers to be called just "Eddie." But he jokes that he is the "E.E.O. of the
Desert." Female Owlingtons are always named Edna. The middle initial E stands
for Elf for both males and females.

Eddie's nest is in an old woodpecker hole. The hole is high in the trunk of a
giant saguaro cactus. It's the perfect spot for a watcher. Eddie has excellent night
vision. He also has superb hearing. Eddie knows everything that goes on in his
neighborhood.

The Bully

Name: Peppi – A Hemipepsis Wasp – also known as a Tarantula Hawk

Nickname: "T-Hawk" – A nickname that Peppi likes a lot

Size: 2 inches from head to tip of abdomen

Color: Shiny, metallic blue-black body. Four large, reddish-orange wings

Favorite Foods: Adults sip the nectar from brittlebush flowers. Larvae eat the living body of paralyzed

spiders hunted by their mother

Habitat: Dry desert hillsides and rocky scrublands of the Southwest

Peppi is a mean old tarantula hawk wasp. She's the neighborhood bully. She likes to sip the nectar from brittlebush flowers that grow in the desert behind the human's store. But every spring, Peppi goes hunting for big spiders. She even hunts tarantulas. Peppi paralyzes the spider with the venom from her long stinger. Then she drags the spider's body back into its own burrow. She lays a single egg on the body of the living spider. Then she seals the burrow. When the egg hatches a few days later, her wasp larva has a fresh spider to eat... alive.

Words to Learn

aggressive (uh-GRES-iv) Showing a readiness to attack others.

arid (AIR-id) Extremely dry.

burrow (BUHR-oh) A hole in the ground made by an animal.

confrontation (Kuhn-frun-TAY-shun) To meet or face someone or something in a challenging or hostile way.

Day of reckoning (RECK-uh-ning) The time to settle all disputes or accounts.

ectotherms (EK-tuh-thurms) Animals whose body temperature changes when the outside temperature changes. Some people call ectotherms "cold-blooded animals."

larva (LAHR-vuh) A young insect hatched from an egg. Looks like a worm.

molt (MOHLT) To shed old skin, fur, hair or feathers so that new ones can grow.

nocturnal (nok-TURN-el) Active at night. In the desert, pack rats and other animals often rest during the day to avoid the bright sun and hot temperatures. They search for food and are most active after the sun sets.

pincer (PIN-sur) The pinching claw of an insect or arachnid.

predator (PRED-a-tohr) An animal that hunts and eats other animals.

prey (PRAY) Animals that are hunted and eaten by other animals.

saguaro (suh-WARH-oh) A very tall cactus with arms that grows only in the Sonoran Desert of Arizona and northern Mexico.

scorpion (SKOR-pee-uhn) An arachnid related to spiders. Scorpions have a long, jointed body that ends in a long tail tipped with a venomous stinger.

sneer (SNEER) To smile in a hateful or hostile way.

tarantula (tuh-RAN-chuh-luh) A large, hairy spider found mainly in warm regions. It does have fangs with venom, but is not aggressive unless provoked.

taunt (TAWNT) To try to make someone angry or upset by saying unkind things about him or her.

tease (TEEZ) To say unkind things to someone in a way that is meant to be playful. Teasing can also hurt someone's feelings.

venom (VEH-nuhm) Poison. Tarantulas inject venom with their fangs when they bite. Scorpions inject venom with the stinger on the tip of their tail. The venom kills insects and other prey.

CONRAD J. STORAD is the national award-winning author of more than 40 science and nature books for young readers. He has lived in Arizona's Sonoran Desert since 1982. Many of Storad's books reflect his interest and fascination with the plants and animals that live there. His book Arizona Way Out West & Wacky won the 2012 Benjamin Franklin Silver Medal Award for best children's nonfiction. In 2011, USA Book News gave his Rattlesnake Rules a Best Book Award for children's nonfiction. Storad has written and edited many award-winning picture books distributed by Bobolink Media, including *Desert Night Shift, Life in the Slow Lane, Lizards for Lunch, Don't Ever Cross That Road*, and *Don't Call Me Pig! (A Javelina Story)*. Conrad and is wife Laurie live in Tempe, Arizona with Sophia, their miniature black and tan, double dapple dachshund. Together, they enjoy exploring the nooks and crannies of Arizona and beautiful places across the American Southwest.

Illustrator of our titles: *Life in the Slow Lane, Don't Ever Cross That Road, Desert Night Shift* and *Big Horns Don't Honk*. **NATHANIEL P. JENSEN** grew up in Austin, Texas, attending Pflugerville Schools and obtaining a BFA from the University of Texas at Austin. Since 1990 he has been a working artist in Austin, where as a public artist he has painted murals as tall as 60 feet; as an illustrator he has created award-winning graphic illustrations for national, state and city publications; as a painter he has exhibited in venues large and small throughout the city; and as an art activist he has worked passionately to bring Austin arts to the forefront of community consciousness.